A MESSAGE FROM JUST WILLIAM

'Lo everywun. (I think that's spelt krektly . . .)

I'm jolly pleased that ol' Virgin Trains is giving out *Meet Just William* in their goody bags. They're really funny stories 'bout me an' my adventures. With some fab drawings by Tony Ross as well.

My favourite story is prob'ly the one called 'The Christmas Truce', where I get revenge on my sworn enemy, Hubert Lane. That's when I swap round all the presents and me and my Outlaws get the best stuff.

Another good one is 'William and the Musician', which starts with me thinkin' I'm the ruler of the whole world. Well, I like doin' good, ritin' wrongs – and pursuin' happiness. Cos that's important. Like in 'William Leads a Better Life'. Doesn't always go according to plan though.

An' 'William's Birthday' is a brilliant tail – sorry, I mean 'tale' – 'bout how I meet two triffic dogs when I've been forced to go to a borin' old dancin' class.

I like trains. And planes. An' I wouldn't mind goin' hot-air balloonin' one day. My elder brother, Robert, says I'm full of hot air, but that's just stupid.

Anyway, have a great time, wherever you're off to. An' enjoy my book. I bet you laugh too.

Happy Christmas!

From WILLIAM BROWN and MARTIN JARVIS

KT-555-965

William's Birthday and Other Stories

Richmal Crompton, who wrote the original *Just William* stories, was born in Lancashire in 1890. The first story about William Brown appeared in *Home* magazine in 1919, and the first collection of William stories was published in book form three years later. In all, thirty-eight William books were published, the last one in 1970, after Richmal Crompton's death.

Martin Jarvis, who has adapted the stories in this book for younger readers, first discovered *Just William* when he was nine years old. He made his first adaptation of a William story for BBC radio in 1973 and since then his broadcast readings have become classics in their own right. BBC Worldwide have released nearly a hundred William stories on audio cassette and for these international best-sellers Martin has received a Gold Disc and the British Talkies Award. An award-winning actor, Martin has also appeared in numerous stage plays, television series and films.

Titles in the *Meet Just William* series

William's Birthday and Other Stories
William and the Hidden Treasure and Other Stories
William's Wonderful Plan and Other Stories
William and the Prize Cat and Other Stories
William and the Haunted House and Other Stories

Meet **Just William**

William's Birthday and Other Stories

Adapted from Richmal Crompton's
original stories by Martin Jarvis

Illustrated by Tony Ross

MACMILLAN CHILDREN'S BOOKS

First published 1999 by Macmillan Children's Books
a division of Macmillan Publishers Limited
20 New Wharf Road, London N1 9RR
Basingstoke and Oxford
www.panmacmillan.com

In association with Virgin Trains

ISBN 0 330 39097 X

11 13 15 17 19 18 16 14 12

A CIP catalogue record for this book is available from
the British Library.

Typeset by SX Composing DTP, Rayleigh, Essex
Printed and bound in Great Britain by Mackays of Chatham plc, Kent

Contents

Dear Reader

Ullo. I'm William Brown. Spect you've heard of me an' my dog Jumble cause we're jolly famous on account of all the adventures wot me an' my friends the Outlaws have.

Me an' the Outlaws try an' avoid our famlies cause they don' unnerstan' us. Specially my big brother Robert an' my rotten sister Ethel. She's awful. An' my parents are really <u>hartless</u>. Y'know, my father stops my pocket-money for no reason at all, an' my mother never lets me keep pet rats or <u>anythin'</u>.

It's jolly hard bein' an Outlaw an' havin' adventures when no one unnerstan's you, I can tell you.

You can read all about me, if you like, in this excitin' an' speshul new collexion of all my fav'rite stories. I hope you have a jolly gud time readin' 'em.

Yours truly

William Brown

William's Birthday

It was William's birthday, but, in spite of that, his spirit was gloomy and overcast. He hadn't got Jumble, his beloved mongrel, and a birthday without Jumble was, in William's eyes, a hollow mockery of a birthday.

Jumble had hurt his foot in a rabbit trap, and had been treated for it at home, till William's well-meaning but mistaken ministrations had caused the vet to advise Jumble's removal to his own establishment.

William had indignantly protested, but his family was adamant. And when the question of his birthday celebration was broached, feeling was still high on both sides.

"I'd like a dog for my birthday present," said William.

"You've got a dog," said his mother.

"I shan't have when you an' that man have killed it between you," said William. "He puts on their bandages so tight that their calculations stop flowin' an' that's jus' the same as stranglin' 'em."

"Nonsense, William!"

"Anyway, I want a dog for my birthday present. I'm sick of not havin' a dog. I want another dog. I want two more dogs."

"Nonsense! Of course you can't have another dog."

"I said two more dogs."

"You can't have two more dogs."

"Well, anyway, I needn't go to the dancing-class on my birthday."

The dancing-class was at present the bane of William's life. It took place on Wednesday afternoons – William's half-holiday – and it was an ever-present and burning grievance to him.

He was looking forward to his birthday chiefly because he took for granted that he would be given a holiday from the dancing-class. But it turned out that there, too, Fate was against him.

Of course he must go to the dancing-class, said Mrs Brown. It was only an hour, and it was a most expensive course, and she'd promised that he shouldn't miss a single lesson because Mrs Beauchamp said that he was very slow and clumsy and she really hadn't wanted to take him.

To William it seemed the worst that could

possibly happen to him. But it wasn't. When he heard that Ethel's admirer, Mr Dewar, was coming to tea on his birthday, his indignation rose to boiling point.

"But it's my birthday. I don't want *him* here on my birthday."

William had a deeply rooted objection to Mr Dewar. Mr Dewar had an off-hand, facetious manner which William had disliked from his first meeting with him.

William awoke on the morning of his birthday, still in a mood of unmelting resentment.

He went downstairs morosely to receive his presents.

His mother's present to him was a dozen new handkerchiefs with his initials upon each, his father's a new leather pencil-case. William thanked them with a manner of cynical aloofness of which he was rather proud.

"Now, William," said his mother anxiously, "you'll go to the dancing-class nicely this afternoon, won't you?"

"I'll go the way I gen'rally go to things. I've only got one way of goin' anywhere. I don't know whether it's nice or not."

This brilliant repartee cheered him considerably. But still: no Jumble; a dancing class; *that* man to tea. Gloom closed over him again. Mrs Brown was still looking at him anxiously. She had an uneasy suspicion that he meant to play truant from the dancing-class.

When she saw him in his hat and coat after lunch she said again, "William, you *are* going to the dancing-class, aren't you?"

William walked past her with a short laugh that was wild and reckless and daredevil and bitter and sardonic. It was, in short, a very good laugh, and he was proud of it.

Then he swaggered down the drive, and very ostentatiously turned off in the opposite direction to the direction of his dancing-class. He walked on slowly for some time and then turned and retraced his steps with furtive swiftness.

To do so he had to pass the gate of his home,

but he meant to do this in the ditch so that his mother, who might be still anxiously watching the road for the reassuring sight of his return, should be denied the satisfaction of it.

He could not resist, however, peeping cautiously out of the ditch when he reached the gate, to see if she were watching for him. There was no sign of her, but there was something else that made William rise to his feet, his eyes and mouth wide open with amazement.

There, tied to a tree in the drive near the front door, were two young collies, little more than pups. Two dogs. He'd asked his family for two dogs and here they were. Two dogs. He could hardly believe his eyes.

His heart swelled with gratitude and affection for his family. How he'd misjudged them! Thinking they didn't care two pins about his birthday, and here they'd got him the two dogs he'd asked for as a surprise, without saying anything to him about it. Just put them there for him to find.

His heart still swelling with love and gratitude, he went up the drive. The church clock struck the hour. He'd only just be in time for the dancing-class now, even if he ran all the way.

His mother had wanted him to be in time for the dancing-class and the sight of the two dogs had touched his heart so deeply that he wanted to do something in return, to please his mother.

He'd hurry off to the dancing-class at once, and wait till he came back to thank them for the dogs.

He stooped down, undid the two leads from the tree, and ran off again down the drive. The two dogs leapt joyfully beside him.

The smaller collie began to direct his energies to burrowing in the ditches, and the larger one to squeezing through the hedge, where he found himself, to his surprise, in a field of sheep.

He did not know that they were sheep. It was his first day in the country. He had only that morning left a London shop. But dim instincts began to stir in him.

William, watching with mingled consternation and delight, saw him round up the sheep in the field and begin to drive them pell-mell through the hedge into the road; then, hurrying, snapping, barking, drive the whole jostling perturbed flock of them down the road towards William's house.

William stood and watched the proceedings. The delight it afforded him was tempered with apprehension.

The collie had now made his way into a third field, in search of recruits, while his main army waited for him meekly in the road. William hastily decided to dissociate himself from the proceedings entirely. Better to let one of his dogs go than risk losing both . . .

He hurried on to the dancing-class. Near the front door he tied the collie to a tree with the lead, and entered a room where a lot of little boys – most of whom William disliked intensely – were brushing their hair and changing their shoes.

At last a tinkly little bell rang, and they made their way to the large room where the dancing-class was held. From an opposite door was issuing a bevy of little girls, dressed in fairy-like frills, with white socks and dancing-shoes.

There followed an attendant army of mothers and nurses who had been divesting them of stockings and shoes and outdoor garments.

William greeted these fairy-like beings with his most hideous grimace. The one he disliked most of all (a haughty beauty with auburn curls) was given him as a partner.

"*Need* I have William?" she pleaded. "He's so *awful*."

"I'm not," said William. "I'm no more awful than her."

"Have him for a few minutes, dear," said Mrs Beauchamp, who was tall and majestic and almost incredibly sinuous, "and then I'll let you have someone else."

The dancing-class proceeded on its normal course. William glanced at the clock and sighed. Only five minutes gone. A whole hour of it – and on his birthday. His *birthday*. Even the thought of his two new dogs did not quite wipe out *that* grievance.

"Please may I stop having William now? He's doing the steps all wrong."

William defended himself with spirit.

"I'm doin' 'em right. It's her what's doin' 'em wrong."

Mrs Beauchamp stopped them and gave William another partner – a little girl with untidy hair and a roguish smile. She was a partner more to William's liking, and the dance developed into a competition as to who could tread more often on the other's feet.

It was, of course, a pastime unworthy of a famous Indian Chief, but it was better than dancing. He confided in her.

"It's my birthday today, and I've had two dogs given me."

"*Oo! Lucky!*"

"An' I've got one already, so that makes three. Three dogs I've got."

"Oo, I say! Have you got 'em here?"

"I only brought one. It's in the garden tied to a tree near the door."

"Oo, I'm goin' to look at it when we get round to the window!"

They edged to the window, and the little girl glanced out with interest, and stood, suddenly paralysed with horror, her mouth and eyes wide open. But almost immediately her vocal powers returned to her.

"*Look!*" she said. "Oh, *look!*"

They all crowded to the window.

The collie had escaped from his lead and found his way into the little girls' dressing-room.

There he had collected the stockings, shoes, and navy-blue knickers that lay about and brought them all out on to the lawn, where he was happily engaged in worrying them.

Remnants lay everywhere about him. He was tossing up into the air one leg of a pair of navy-blue knickers. Around him the air was thick with wool and fluff. Bits of unravelled stockings, with here and there a dismembered hat, lay about on the lawn in glorious confusion.

He was having the time of his life.

After a moment's frozen horror the whole dancing-class – little girls, little boys, nurses, mothers, and dancing-mistress – surged out on to the lawn.

The collie saw them coming and leapt up playfully, half a pair of knickers hanging out of one corner of his mouth, and a stocking out of the other.

They bore down upon him in a crowd. He wagged his tail in delight. All these people coming to play with him!

He entered into the spirit of the game at once and leapt off to the shrubbery, followed by all these jolly people. A glorious game! The best fun he'd had for weeks . . .

Meanwhile William was making his way

quietly homeward. They'd say it was all his fault, of course, but he'd learnt by experience that it was best to get as far as possible away from the scene of a crime . . .

He turned the bend in the road that brought his own house in sight, and there he stood as if turned suddenly to stone. He'd forgotten the other dog.

The front garden was a sea of sheep. They covered drive, grass and flower beds. They even stood on the steps that led to the front door. The overflow filled the road outside.

Behind them was the other collie pup, running to and fro, crowding them up still more closely, pursuing truants and bringing them back to the fold.

Having collected the sheep, his instinct had told him to bring them to his master. His master was, of course, the man who had brought him from the shop, not the boy who had taken him for a walk. His master was in this house. He had brought the sheep to his master . . .

His master was, in fact, with Ethel in the drawing-room. Mrs Brown was out and was not expected back till tea-time.

Mr Dewar had not yet told Ethel about the two collies he had brought for her. She'd said last week that she "adored" collies, and he'd decided to bring her a couple of them. He meant to introduce the subject quite carelessly, at the right moment.

And so, when she told him that he seemed to understand her better than any other man she'd ever met (she said this to all her admirers in turn), he said to her quite casually, "Oh! By the way, I forgot to mention it but I just bought a little present – or rather presents – for you this afternoon. They're in the drive."

Ethel's face lit up with pleasure and interest.

"Oh, how perfectly sweet of you," she said.

"Have a look at them, and see if you like them."

She walked over to the window. He remained in his armchair, watching the back

of her Botticelli neck, lounging at his ease –
the gracious, all-providing male. She looked
out. Sheep – hundreds and thousands of sheep
– filled the drive, the lawn, the steps, the road
outside.

"Well," said Mr Dewar, "do you like
them?"

She raised a hand to her head.

"What are they for?" she said faintly.

"Pets," said Mr Dewar.

"*Pets!*" she screamed. "I've nowhere to

keep them. I've nothing to feed them on."

"Oh, they only want a few dog biscuits."

"*Dog* biscuits?"

Ethel stared at them wildly for another second, then collapsed on to the nearest chair in hysterics.

Mrs Brown had returned home. Mrs Brown had had literally to fight her way to the front door through a tightly packed mass of sheep.

Mr Dewar was wildly apologetic. He couldn't think what had happened. He couldn't think where the sheep had come from.

The other dog arrived at the same moment as a crowd of indignant farmers demanding their sheep. It still had a knicker hanging out of one corner of its mouth and a stocking out of the other.

William was nowhere to be seen.

William came home about half an hour later. There were no signs of Mr Dewar, or the dogs, or the sheep. Ethel and Mrs Brown were in the drawing-room.

"I shall never speak to him again," Ethel was saying. "I don't care whether it was his fault or not. I've told him never to come to the house again."

"I don't think he'd dare to when your father's seen the state the grass is in. It looks like a ploughed field."

"As if I'd want hundreds of *sheep* like that," said Ethel, still confusing what Mr Dewar had meant to do with what he had actually done. "*Pets* indeed!"

"And Mrs Beauchamp's just rung up about the other dog," went on Mrs Brown. "It evidently followed William to the dancing-class and tore up some stockings and things there. I don't see how she can blame us for that. She really was very rude about it. I don't think I shall let William go to any more of her dancing-classes."

William sat listening with an expressionless face, but his heart was singing within him. No more dancing classes . . . that man never coming to the house any more. A glorious birthday – except for one thing, of course.

But just then the housemaid came into the room.

"Please, 'm, it's the man from the vet with Master William's dog. He says he's quite all right now."

William leapt from the room, and he and Jumble fell upon each other ecstatically in the hall. The minute he saw Jumble, William knew that he could never have endured to have any other dog.

"I'll take him for a little walk. I bet he wants one."

The joy of walking along the road again, with his beloved Jumble at his heels. William's heart was full of dreamy content.

He'd got Jumble back. That man was never coming to the house any more.

He wasn't going to any more dancing-classes.

It was the nicest birthday he'd ever had in his life.

The Christmas Truce

It was Hubert Lane's mother's idea that the Outlaws versus Hubert Laneites feud should be abolished.

"Christmas, you know," she said vaguely to William's mother, "the season of peace and good will. If they don't bury the hatchet at this season, they never will. It's so absurd for them to go on like this. Think how much *happier* they'd be if they were *friends*."

Mrs Brown murmured, "Er – yes," and Mrs Lane continued, "I've thought out how to do it. If you'll invite Hubie to Willie's party, we'll *insist* on his coming, and we'll invite Willie to Hubie's and you *insist* on his coming, and then it will be all right. They'll have got to know each other, and, I'm sure, have learnt to love each other."

Mrs Brown said, "Er – yes" again, because she couldn't think of anything else to say, and so the matter was settled.

When it was broached to William, he was speechless with horror.

"*Him?*" he exploded fiercely, when at last the power of speech returned to him. "Ask *him* to my Christmas party? I'd sooner not have a Christmas party at all than ask *him* to it. *Him!* Well then, I jolly well won't have a party at all."

But William's tempestuous fury was as usual of no avail against his mother's gentle firmness.

"William," she said. "I've promised."

She sent an invitation to Hubert Lane and to Bertie Franks (Hubert's friend and lieutenant) and to Hubert's other friends, and they all accepted in their best copperplate handwriting.

William and his Outlaws went about sunk deep in gloom.

"If it wasn't for the trifle an' the crackers," said William darkly, "I wouldn't have had it at all – not with *him*."

His mood grew darker and darker as the day approached. The prospect of the end of the feud brought no glow of joy to the Outlaws' hearts. Without the Hubert Lane feud, life would be dull indeed.

The Outlaws and their supporters – as arranged – arrived first, and stood round William like a bodyguard, awaiting the arrival of the Hubert Laneites.

They wore perfectly blank expressions, prepared to meet the Hubert Laneites in whatever guise they presented themselves. And the guise in which they ultimately presented themselves was worse than the Outlaws' worst fears.

They advanced upon their host with an oily friendliness that was nauseating. They winked at each other openly. They said, "Thanks *so* much for asking us, William. It was ripping of you. Oh, I say . . . what *topping* decorations!"

And they nudged each other and sniggered.

Mrs Brown, of course, was deceived by their show of friendliness.

"There, William," she whispered triumphantly, "I knew it would be all right. I'm sure you'll be the *greatest* friends after this. His mother *said* he was a nice little boy."

William did not reply to this because there wasn't anything he could trust himself to say.

They went in to tea.

"Oh, I say, how *ripping*! How *topping*!" said the Hubert Laneites gushingly to Mrs

Brown, nudging each other and sniggering whenever her eye was turned away from them.

Once Hubert looked at William and made his most challenging grimace, turning immediately to Mrs Brown to say with an ingratiating smile, "It's a simply topping party, Mrs Brown, and it's awfully nice of you to ask us."

Mrs Brown beamed at him and said, "It's so nice to *have* you, Hubert," and the other Hubert Laneites sniggered.

William kept his hands in his pockets with such violence that one of them went right through the lining.

But the crowning catastrophe happened when they pulled the crackers.

Hubert went up to William and said, "See what I've got out of a cracker, William," and held up a ring that sent a squirt of water into William's face.

The Hubert Laneites went into paroxysms of silent laughter. Hubert was all smirking contrition.

"I say, I'm so sorry, William, I'd no idea that it would do that. I just got it out of one of the crackers. I say, I'm so sorry, William."

It was evident to everyone but Mrs Brown that the ring had not come out of a cracker, but had been carefully brought by Hubert in order to play this trick on William.

William was wiping water out of his eyes and ears.

"It's quite all right, dear," said Mrs Brown. "It was *quite* an accident, we all saw. They shouldn't have such nasty things in crackers, but it wasn't your fault. Tell him that you don't mind a bit, William."

But William hastily left the room.

The rest of the party passed off uneventfully. The Hubert Laneites said goodbye at the end with nauseous gratitude and went sniggering down the drive.

"*There*, William!" said Mrs Brown as she shut the door. "I knew it would be all right. They were so grateful and they enjoyed it *so* much and you're *quite* friends now, aren't you?"

But William was already upstairs in his bedroom, pummelling his bolster with such energy that he burst his collar open.

During the days that intervened between William's party and Hubert Lane's party, the Hubert Laneites kept carefully out of the way of the Outlaws. Yet the Outlaws felt uneasily that something was brewing.

"We've gotter do somethin' to them at their

party, same as they did to us at ours," said Ginger firmly.

"Yes, but what can we do?" said William. "We can't start fightin' 'em. We've promised not to. An' – an' there's nothin' else we *can* do. Jus' wait, jus' *wait* till their party's over."

"But they'll never forget that water squirt," said Ginger mournfully.

"Unless we do somethin' back," said Douglas.

"What can we do in *their* house, with them watchin' us all the time?" said Henry.

"We mus' jus' *think*," said William. "There's four days an' we'll think hard."

But the day of Hubert's party arrived, and they'd thought of nothing.

They met in the old barn in the morning to arrange their plan of action, but none of them could think of any plan of action to arrange.

William walked slowly and draggingly through the village on his way home to lunch. His mother had told him to stop at the baker's with an order for her, and it was a sign of his intense depression that he remembered to do it.

He entered the baker's shop. It seemed to be full of people. Then he suddenly realised that the mountainous lady just in front of him was Mrs Lane.

She was talking in a loud voice to a friend.

"Yes, Hubie's party is this afternoon. We're having William Brown and his friends. To put a stop to that silly quarrel that's gone on so long. Hubie's so lovable that I simply can't think how anyone could quarrel with him.

But of course it will be all right after today.

"We're having a Father Christmas, you know. Bates, our gardener, is going to be the Father Christmas and give out presents. I've given Hubie three pounds to get some *really* nice presents for it to celebrate the ending of the feud."

William waited his turn, gave his message, and went home for lunch.

Immediately after lunch, he made his way to Bates's cottage, which stood on the road at the end of the Lanes' garden.

William approached the cottage with great circumspection, looking around to make sure that none of the Hubert Laneites was in sight.

He opened the gate, walked up the path, and knocked at the door, standing poised on one foot ready to turn to flee should Bates, recognising him – and remembering some of his former exploits in his kitchen garden – attack him on sight.

He heaved a sigh of relief, however, when Bates opened the door. It was clear that Bates did not recognise him – he merely received him with an ungracious scowl.

"Well?" said Bates. "What d'you want?"

William assumed an ingratiating smile, the smile of a boy who has every right to demand admittance to the cottage.

"I say," he said, with a fairly good imitation of the Hubert Laneites' most patronising manner, "you've got the Father Christmas things here, haven't you?"

The ungraciousness of Bates's scowl did not relax. He had been pestered to death over the Father Christmas things.

He took for granted that William was one of the Hubert Laneites, coming once more to "muss up" his bag of parcels, and take one out, or put one in, or snigger over them, as they'd been doing every day for the last week.

"Yes," he said, "I've got the things 'ere an' they're all right, so there's no call to start upsettin' of 'em again. I've had enough of you comin' in an' mussin' the place up."

"I only wanted to count them, and make

31

sure that we've got the right number," said William with an oily friendliness that was worthy of Hubert himself.

"All right, go in an' count 'em. I tell you, I'm sick of the whole lot of you, I am." And Bates waved him irascibly into the back parlour.

William entered, and threw a quick glance out of the window. Yes, Ginger was there, as they had arranged he should be, hovering near the shed where the apples were sorted.

Then he looked round the room. A red cloak and hood and white beard were spread out on the sofa, and on the hearthrug lay a sackful of small parcels.

William fell on his knees and began to make pretence of counting the parcels. Suddenly, he looked up and gazed out of the window.

"I say!" he said. "There's a boy taking your apples."

Bates leapt to the window. There, upon the roof of the shed, was Ginger, with an arm through the open window, obviously in the act of purloining apples.

With a yell of fury, Bates sprang to the door and down the path towards the shed. Left alone, William turned his attention quickly to the sack. It contained parcels, each one labelled and named.

He had to act quickly. He had no time to investigate. He had to act solely upon his suspicions and his knowledge of the characters of Hubert and his friends.

Quickly, he began to change the labels of the little parcels. Just as he was fastening the last one, Bates returned, hot and breathless,

having failed to catch the nimble Ginger.

"Now you clear out," he said. "I'm sick of the lot of you."

Smiling the patronising smile of a Laneite, William took a hurried departure, and ran home as quickly as he could to change.

The Hubert Laneites received the Outlaws with even more nauseous friendliness than they had shown at William's house.

It was evident, however, from the way they sniggered and nudged each other that they had some plan prepared. William felt anxious. Suppose that the plot they had so obviously prepared had nothing to do with the Father Christmas . . .

They went into the hall after tea, and Mrs Lane said roguishly, "Now, boys, I've got a visitor for you."

Immediately, Bates, inadequately disguised as Father Christmas and looking fiercely resentful of the whole proceedings, entered with his sack.

The Hubert Laneites sniggered delightedly.

This was evidently the crowning moment of the afternoon. Bates took the parcels out one by one, announcing the name on each label.

The first said "William".

The Hubert Laneites watched him go up to receive it in paroxysms of silent mirth. William took it and opened it wearing a sphinx-like expression.

It was the most magnificent mouth organ that he had ever seen. The mouths of the Hubert Laneites dropped in horror and amazement. It was evidently the present that Hubert had destined for himself.

Bates called out Hubert's name. Hubert, his mouth still hanging open with horror and amazement, went to receive his parcel.

It contained a short pencil with a shield and rubber, of the sort that can be purchased for a penny or twopence. He went back to his seat, blinking.

He examined his label. It bore his name. He examined William's label. It bore William's name. There was no mistake about it.

William was thanking Mrs Lane effusively for his present. "Yes, dear," she was saying, "I'm so glad you like it. I haven't had time to look at them, but I told Hubie to get nice things."

Hubert opened his mouth to protest, and then shut it again. He was beaten and he knew it.

He couldn't very well tell his mother that he'd spent the bulk of the money on the presents for himself and his particular friends, and had spent only a few coppers on the Outlaws' presents. He couldn't think what had happened.

Meanwhile, the presentation was going on. Bertie Franks' present was a ruler that could not have cost more than a penny, and Ginger's was a magnificent electric torch.

Bertie stared at the torch with an expression that would have done credit to a tragic mask, and Ginger hastened to establish permanent right to his prize by going up to thank Mrs Lane for it.

"Yes, it's lovely, dear," she said. "I told Hubie to get nice things."

Douglas's present was a splendid penknife, and Henry's a fountain pen, while the corresponding presents for the Hubert Laneites were an indiarubber and a notebook.

The Hubert Laneites watched their presents passing into their enemies' hands with expressions of helpless agony.

But Douglas's parcel had more than a penknife in it. It had a little bunch of imitation flowers with an indiarubber bulb attached, and a tiny label saying, "Show this to William and press the rubber thing."

Douglas took it to Hubert. Hubert knew what it was, of course, for he had bought it, but he was paralysed with horror at the whole situation.

"Look, Hubert," said Douglas.

A fountain of ink caught Hubert neatly in the eye. Douglas was all surprise and contrition.

"I'm so sorry, Hubert," he said. "I'd no idea

that it was going to do that. I've just got it out of my parcel and I'd no idea that it was going to do that. I'm so sorry, Mrs Lane. I'd no idea that it was going to do that."

"Of course you hadn't, dear," said Mrs Lane. "It's Hubie's own fault for buying a thing like that. It's very foolish of him indeed."

Hubert wiped the ink out of his eyes and sputtered helplessly.

Then William discovered that it was time to go.

"Thank you so much for our lovely presents, Hubert," he said, politely. "We've had a *lovely* time."

And Hubert, under his mother's eye, smiled a green and sickly smile.

The Outlaws marched triumphantly down the road, brandishing their spoils. William was playing on his mouth organ, Ginger was flashing his electric torch, Henry was waving his fountain pen, and Douglas was slashing at the hedge with his penknife.

Occasionally they turned round to see if

their enemies were pursuing them, but the Hubert Laneites were too broken in spirit to enter into open hostilities just then.

As they walked, the Outlaws raised a wild and inharmonious paean of triumph.

And at that moment over the telephone, Mrs Lane was saying to Mrs Brown, "Yes, dear, it's been a *complete* success. They're the *greatest* friends now. I'm sure it's been a Christmas that they'll all remember all their lives."

William Leads a Better Life

If you go far enough back, it was William's form master who was responsible for the whole thing.

Mr Strong had set for homework more French than it was convenient for William to learn. Who would waste the precious hours of a summer evening over French verbs? Certainly not William.

In the morning, however, things somehow seemed different. William lay in bed and considered the matter.

"Mother, I don't think I feel quite well enough to go to school this morning," he called faintly.

41

Mrs Brown entered the room looking distressed. She smoothed his pillow.

"Poor little boy," she said tenderly. "Where's the pain?"

"All over," said William, playing for safety.

But the patient's father, when summoned, was having none of it.

"You'd better get up as quickly as you can. You'll be late for school. And doubtless they'll know how to deal with *that*."

They did know how to deal with that. They knew too how to deal with William's complete ignorance on the subject of French verbs.

He went home to lunch embittered and disillusioned with life. On the way, Ginger, Henry and Douglas began to discuss the history lesson.

The history master had given them a graphic account of the life of St Francis of Assisi. William had paid little attention, but Ginger remembered it all. William began to follow the discussion.

"Yes, but why'd he do it?" he said.

"Well, he jus' got kind of fed up with things, an' he had visions an' things, an' he took some things of his father's to sell to get money to start it—"

"*Crumbs!* Wasn't his father mad?"

"Yes, but that di'n't matter. He was a saint, was Saint Francis, so he could sell his father's things if he liked, an' he 'n' his frien's took the money and got long sort of clothes, an' went an' lived away in a little house by themselves, an' he use' ter preach to animals, an' to people, an' call everythin' 'brother' an' 'sister' an' they cooked all their own stuff to eat an'—"

"Jolly fine it sounds," said William enviously. "An' did their people let 'em?"

"They couldn't stop 'em," said Ginger. "An' Francis – he was the head one – an' the others all called themselves Franciscans, an' they built churches an' things."

They had reached the gate of William's house now, and William turned in slowly.

Lunch increased still further William's grievances. No one enquired after his health, though he tried to look pale and ill, and refused a second helping of rice pudding with a meaningful, "No thank you, not today. I would if I felt all right, thank you very much."

Even that elicited no anxious enquiries.

No one, thought William, as he finished up the rice pudding in secret in the larder afterwards, no one else in the world, surely, had such a callous family. It would just serve them right if he went off like St Francis and never came back.

He met Henry and Ginger and Douglas again as usual on the way to afternoon school.

"I've been thinkin' a lot about that saint man. I'd a lot sooner be a saint than keep goin' to school an' learnin' things like French verbs without any *sense* in them. I'd much sooner be a saint, wun't you?"

The other Outlaws looked doubtful.

"They wun't let us," said Henry.

"They can't stop us bein' saints," said William piously, "an' doin' good, an' preachin' – not if we have visions. An' I feel as if I could have visions quite easy."

The Outlaws had slackened their pace.

"What'd we have to do first?" said Ginger.

"Sell some of our fathers' things to get money," said William firmly. "Then we find a place, an' get the right sort of clothes to wear – sort of long things—"

"Dressing-gowns'd do," said Douglas.

"All right," said William.

"Where'll we live?" said Henry.

"We oughter build a place, but till we've

45

built it, we can live in the old barn," said William.

"An what'll we be called? We can't be the Outlaws now we're saints, I s'pose?"

"What were they called?"

"Franciscans . . . After Francis – he was the head one."

"Well, if there's goin' to be any head one," said William, "I'm goin' to be him."

None of them denied to William the position of leader. It was his by right. He had always led, and he was a leader they were proud to follow.

"Well, they just put 'cans' on to the end of his name," said Henry. "Franciscans. So we'll be Williamcans—"

"Sounds kind of funny," said Ginger dubiously.

"I think it sounds jolly fine," said William proudly.

The first meeting of the "Williamcans" was held directly after breakfast the next morning, on Saturday, in the old barn. They had all left notes, dictated by William, on their bedroom mantelpieces, announcing that they were now saints and had left home for ever.

They inspected the possessions that they had looted from their unsuspecting fathers: William had appropriated a pair of slippers, Douglas an inkstand, Ginger had two ties, and Henry a pair of gloves.

They looked at their spoils with proud satisfaction.

"We'd better not put on our saint robes yet – not till we've been down to the village to sell the things. Then we'll put 'em on an' start preachin' an' things. An', remember – from now on, we've gotter call each other 'Saint' an' call everythin' else 'brother' or 'sister'."

"*Everything?*"

"Yes – *he* did – the other man did."

"Yes, but William—"

"You've gotter call me St William now, Ginger."

"All right. You call me St Ginger."

"All right, I'm goin' to, St Ginger—"

"St William."

"All right."

"Well, where you goin' to sell the slippers?"

"*Brother* slippers," corrected William. "Well, I'm goin' to sell brother slippers at Mr Marsh's, if he'll buy 'em."

"And I'll take brother ties along too," said Ginger. "And Henry take brother gloves and Douglas, brother inkstand."

"Sister inkstand," said Douglas. "William said—"

"St William," corrected William patiently.

"Well, St William said we could call things brother or sister, and my inkstand's going to be sister."

"Swank," said St Ginger severely. "Always wanted to be diff'rent from other people."

Mr Marsh kept a second-hand shop at the end of the village. He refused to allow them more than sixpence each.

"Mean!" exploded St William indignantly, as soon as they'd emerged from Mr Marsh's dingy little sanctum.

"I suppose now we're saints," said St Ginger piously, "that we've gotter forgive folks what wrong us like that."

"Huh! I'm not going to be that sort of saint," said St William firmly.

Back at the barn, they donned their dressing-gowns.

"Now what do we do first?" said St Ginger.

"Preachin' to animals," said William. "Let's go across to Jenks's farm an' try on them."

They crept rather cautiously into the farmyard.

"I'll do brother cows," said St William, "an' St Ginger do brother pigs, an' St Douglas do brother goats, an' St Henry do sister hens."

They approached their various audiences. Ginger leant over the pigsty. Then he turned to William, who was already striking an attitude before his congregation of cows, and said, "I say, what've I gotter *say* to 'em?"

At that moment, brother goat, being approached too nearly by St Douglas, butted the saintly stomach, and St Douglas sat down suddenly and heavily.

Brother goat, evidently enjoying this form of entertainment, returned to the charge. St Douglas fled, to the accompaniment of an uproarious farmyard commotion.

Farmer Jenks appeared, and, seeing his old

enemies, the Outlaws, actually within his precincts, he uttered a yell of fury and darted down upon them.

The saints fled swiftly, St Douglas holding up his too-flowing robe as he went. Brother goat had given St Douglas a good start, and he reached the barn first.

"Well," said St William, panting, "I've *finished* with preachin' to animals. They must have changed a good bit since *his* time. That's all *I* can say."

"Well, what'll we do *now*?" said Ginger.

"I should almost think it's time for dinner," said William.

It was decided that Douglas and Henry should go down to the village to purchase provisions for the meal. It was decided also that they should go in their dressing-gowns.

For their midday meal, the two saints purchased a large bag of chocolate creams, another of bull's-eyes, and, to form the more solid part of the meal, four cream buns.

Ginger and William were sitting comfortably in the old barn when the two emissaries returned.

"*We've* had a nice time!" exploded St Henry. "All the boys in the place runnin' after us an' shoutin' at us. Douglas has tore his robe and I've fallen in the mud in mine."

"Well, they've gotter last you all the rest of your life," said St William, "so you oughter take more care of 'em," and he added with more interest, "What've you got for dinner?"

When they had eaten, they rested for a short time from their labours.

"I s'pose they *know* now at home that we've gone for good," said Henry with a sigh.

Ginger looked out of the little window anxiously.

"Yes. I only hope to goodness they won't come an' try to fetch us back," he said.

But he need not have troubled. Each family thought that the missing member was having lunch with one of the others and felt no anxiety, only a great relief.

And none of the notes upon the mantelpieces had been found.

"What'll we do *now*?" said William.

"*They* built a church," said Ginger.

"Well, come on," said William, "let's see 'f we can find any stones lyin' about."

They wandered down the road. They still wore their dressing-gowns, but they wore them with a sheepish air.

Fortunately, the road was deserted. They looked up and down, then St Ginger gave a yell of triumph.

The road was being mended, and there by

the roadside, among other materials, lay a little heap of bricks. Moreover, the bricks were unattended. It was the workman's dinner hour.

"Crumbs!" said the Williamcans in delight.

They fell upon the bricks and bore them off in triumph. Soon they had a pile of them just outside the barn where they had resolved to build the church.

But as they paid their last visit for bricks, they met a little crowd of other children, who burst into loud, jeering cries.

"Look at 'em . . . dear little girlies . . . wearin' nice long pinnies . . . oh my! Oh, *don'* they look sweet? Hello, little darlin's!"

William flung aside his saintly robe and fought with the leader. The other saints fought with the others. The saints, smaller in number and size than the other side, most decidedly got the best of it, though not without many casualties.

The other side took to its heels.

St William picked his robe up from the mud

and began to put it on. "Don' see much *sense* in wearin' these things," he said.

"You ought to have *preached* to 'em, not fought 'em," said Ginger severely.

"Well, I bet *he* wun't have preached to 'em if they'd started makin' fun of him. He'd've fought 'em all right."

"No, he wun't," said Ginger firmly. "He di'n't believe in fightin'."

"Well, anyway," said William, "let's get a move on buildin' that church."

They returned to the field.

But the workman had also returned from his dinner hour.

With lurid oaths he tracked them down, and came upon the saints just as they had laboriously laid the first row of bricks for the first wall. He burst upon them with fury.

They did not stay to argue. They fled. Henry cast aside his splendid robe of multi-coloured bath towelling into a ditch to accelerate his flight. The workman tired first, after throwing a brick at their retreating forms.

The Williamcans gathered together dejectedly in the barn.

"Seems to me," said William, "it's a *wearin'* kind of life."

It was cold. It had begun to rain.

"Brother rain," said Ginger brightly.

"Yes, an' I should think it's about sister tea-time," said William. "An' what we goin' to buy it – her – with? How're we goin' to get money?"

They thought deeply for a minute.

"Well," said William at last, voicing the

opinion of the whole order, "I'm jus' about sick of bein' a saint."

The rest looked relieved.

"Yes, I've had *enough*," said William. "There's no *sense* in it. An' I'm almost dyin' of cold and hunger an' I'm goin' home."

They set off homeward, cold and wet and bruised and very hungry. The saintly repast, though enjoyable at the time, had proved singularly unsustaining.

But their troubles were not over.

As they went through the village, they

stopped in front of Mr Marsh's shop window.

There in the very middle were William's father's slippers, Douglas's father's inkstand, Ginger's father's tie, and Henry's father's gloves – all marked at one shilling.

The hearts of the Williamcans stood still. The thought of their fathers seeing their prized possessions reposing in Mr Marsh's window, marked one shilling, was a horrid one.

It had not seemed to matter this morning. This morning, they were leaving their homes for ever. It did seem to matter this evening. This evening, they were returning to their homes.

They entered the shop and demanded them. Mr Marsh was adamant. In the end, Henry fetched his sixpence, William a treasured penknife, Ginger a compass, and Douglas a broken steam engine, and their paternal possessions were handed back.

They went home, dejectedly through the rain.

William discovered with relief that his

father had not yet come home. He found his note unopened still upon the mantelpiece. He tore it up. He tidied himself superficially. He went downstairs.

"Had a nice day, dear?" said his mother.

He disdained to answer the question.

"There's just an hour before tea," she went on. "Hadn't you better be doing your homework, dear?"

He considered. One might as well drink of tragedy to the very dregs while one was about it. It would be a rotten ending to a rotten day.

Besides, there was no doubt about it, Mr Strong was going to make himself very disagreeable indeed if he didn't know those French verbs for Monday. He might as well . . .

If he'd had any idea how rotten it was being a saint, he jolly well wouldn't have wasted a whole Saturday over it. He took down a French grammar and sat down moodily before it, without troubling to put it the right way up.

William and the Musician

William sat on the crest of the hill, his chin cupped in his hands. He surveyed the expanse of country that swept out before him and, as he surveyed it, he became the owner of all the land and houses as far as he could see.

Finding the confines even of England too cramping for him, he became the ruler of the whole world.

He made sweeping and imperious gestures with his right arm – gestures that sent his servants on missions to the farthest ends of the earth.

It was at this point that William realised he

was not alone. A small man had climbed the hill and now sat watching him with interest. Near the small man was a large pack.

"Well, did you catch it?" said the small man pleasantly, as William turned to meet his eye.

"Catch what?" said William.

"The mosquito. I thought you got him that last grab."

"Yes, I got him all right," said William coldly. He swept his arm around in another circle and added, "All that land belongs to me. It's mine as far as you can see."

The man had a brown, humorous but sad face. He looked impressed.

"But you're under age, of course. I suppose you have a guardian or an agent of some sort to manage it for you."

"Oh yes," said William. "Oh yes, I have a guardian or agent all right."

"Your parents are both dead, of course?" the man said.

"Oh yes," said William. "Oh yes, my parents are both dead all right."

"And where do you live?"

The most imposing house within sight was the Hall.

William pointed to it.

"I live there," he said.

As a matter of fact, the Hall was rather in the public eye at present. Mr Bott (of Bott's Sauce) lived there, and Mrs Bott had recently given a staggering subscription to the rebuilding of Marleigh Cottage Hospital.

The result of this was that the Chairman

of the Hospital, Lord Faversham, was coming down from London to attend a party at the Hall to which the entire neighbourhood – including the Browns – was invited, and which was to assure for ever Mrs Bott's place among the neighbouring aristocracy.

William had heard nothing else mentioned in the village for days past.

"I'm giving a large party there next Friday," he said nonchalantly. "Lord Faversham's coming to it, and a lot more dukes and earls and things."

William suddenly caught sight of a little dog lying on the ground behind the pack, fast asleep.

"I say," he said, "is that your dog?"

"Yes," said the little man, "it's Toby. Wake up, Toby. Show the gentleman what you can do, Toby."

Toby woke up and showed the gentleman what he could do. He could walk on his hind legs and dance and shoulder a stick and pace up and down like a sentry. William watched him ecstatically.

"I say! I've never *seen* such a clever dog!"

"Never *was* such a dog," said the little man. "But do people want him? No. Punch and Judy's out of date, they say. I don't know what the world's coming to."

William's eyes opened still further.

"You got a Punch and Judy show?" he said.

The man nodded and pointed to his pack on which the faded letters "Signor Manelli" could be faintly seen.

"Yes," he said. "Same as my father before me, though my father never had a dog like Toby."

He was actually an Italian, he said, and had come to England with his father and mother when he was only a few weeks old.

He had never been out of England since, but his ambition was to make enough money to go back to Italy to his father's people. It was an ambition, however, that he had almost given up hope of fulfilling.

"Well, I *like* Punch and Judy," said William, "and if—"

The little man interrupted him, his soft, brown eyes shining. "Listen," he said, "this party you're giving on Friday. Couldn't you engage us for that? I promise that we'd give you our best performance."

"Er – yes," said William flatly. "Yes, of course."

"I'll come then? What time does the party begin?"

"Er – three o'clock," said William, struggling with a nightmarish feeling of horror. "But I'm afraid – you see – I mean—"

"I promise you I won't disappoint your guests. You won't regret it. I thank you from my heart."

He had leapt to his feet and was already shouldering his pack.

"Three o'clock on Friday," he said. "I'll not disappoint you."

Already he was swinging down the hill.

"But – look here – wait a minute . . ."

William called after him, desperately.

But the little man was already out of sight and earshot.

During the next few days William lived in a double nightmare, of which the subject was sometimes the little man arriving full of hope and pride at the Hall on Friday and being summarily dismissed by an enraged Mr Bott, and sometimes himself on whom the hand of retribution would most surely fall.

"They're going to have an entertainment," his mother said at breakfast one morning.

"What sort of entertainment?" said William hopefully.

"Zevrier, the violinist," said Mrs Brown. "He's really *famous*, you know. And *terribly* modern."

"I wonder if . . ." said William tentatively. "I mean, don't you think people would rather have a Punch and Judy show than a violinist?"

"A Punch and Judy show? Don't be so *ridiculous*, William. It's not a children's party."

By the time Friday actually arrived, however, William's natural optimism had reasserted itself. The little man had, of course, taken the whole thing as a joke and would never think of it again.

Still, as William wandered about among the guests, he kept an anxious eye upon the entrance gates.

Lord Faversham, wearing an expression of acute boredom, was being ushered by a perspiring Mrs Bott into the tent where Zevrier's recital was to take place. Then Mrs Bott went to the door to look up and down anxiously for Zevrier.

The tentful of people began to grow restive. It was quarter-past three. The audience didn't particularly want to hear Zevrier, but it had come to hear him and it wanted to get it over.

Mrs Bott, whose large face now rivalled in colour her husband's famous sauce, went into the library where her husband had sought temporary refuge with a stiff whisky and soda.

"Botty, he's not come," she said hysterically.

"Who's not come?" said Mr Bott gloomily.

"Zebra, the violin man. Oh, Botty, what shall I do? They'll all be laughing at me. Oh, Botty, isn't it *awful*!"

Mr Bott shook his head. "I can't help it," he said. "You *would* have all this set-out. I warned you it wouldn't come to no good."

"But, Botty, there they are, all waiting, an'

nothing happening! Can't you *do* something, Botty?"

"What can I do? I can't play the vi'lin . . ."

Meanwhile, outside the tent, William had turned to see a small, pack-laden figure approaching. His heart froze within him.

"Ah, my little host, I am so sorry to be late. The bus broke down. Ah, here are your guests all ready for me. I will waste no more time . . ."

Still speaking, he entered the tent, mounted the little platform that had been prepared for Zevrier, and began to set up his miniature stage.

William stood for a moment, rooted to the ground by sheer horror, then, his courage suddenly failing him, began to run down the drive and along the road that led to his home.

But just as he was rounding the corner of the boundaries of the Hall estate, he ran into the strange figure – a figure wearing an open collar, flowing tie, and shock of long, carefully waved hair. It carried a violin-case. There was no doubt at all – it was Zevrier.

William was going to hasten past, when he noticed the musician's expression – ill tempered, querulous. He remembered the appealing, rather helpless friendliness of the little Punch and Judy man. He imagined the inevitable clash between them.

Again the nightmare closed over him.

"Er – please," he began incoherently.

The musician stopped short and scowled at him. "Yes?"

"Er – are you going to the Hall?"

"Yes," snapped the musician.

"To play to them?"

"Yes."

"Are you Mr Zevrier?"

"I'm Zevrier," said the man, tossing back his hair and striking an attitude.

"Well – well – I wouldn't go to play to them if I was you."

"Why not?" snapped the musician.

William silently considered this question.

"Well, I wouldn't," he said mysteriously, "if I was you. That's all."

The musician was feeling particularly annoyed that afternoon. He was engaged in writing his autobiography, and he could not find anything interesting to put into it. He wanted it to abound in picturesque episodes, and he couldn't find even one picturesque episode to put into it.

Moreover, he disliked Mrs Bott, though he had never met her. She began all her letters to him, "Dear Mr Zebra".

"Pigs!" he burst out suddenly. "Buying immortal genius by the hour, as if it were tape at so much a yard."

"Yes," said William, "yes, that's just what I think about it."

"*You!*" said the musician, glaring at him. "How can *you* understand?"

"I *do* understand," said William fervently. "I – well, I do understand. I mean, you tell me a bit more what you feel about it. I – I mean, I want to *know* what you feel about it."

William's attitude was that every word postponed the inevitable moment of reckoning.

"You – you don't know what music is to me," said the musician striking his chest dramatically.

"Yes, I do," said William.

Experience had taught him that with a little care and skill, any argument can be prolonged almost indefinitely.

"*You* don't love music."

"Yes, I do."

"It isn't – life and breath to you."

73

"Yes, it is."

The musician looked at William closely. William's expression was guileless and innocent. He could not know, of course, that William was probably the most unmusical boy in the British Empire.

"Suppose," said the musician, tossing back his long hair, "suppose I played to you instead, would it be something that you'd remember all your life?"

"*Yes*," said William, fixing an idiotic smile upon his lips.

"I will," said the musician, already beginning to compose the episode – with picturesque additions – in his mind. "Let us go—"

His gaze rested on a haystack in a field next to the road. That would look well in a book of memoirs. Perhaps some artist would even be inspired to paint the scene. With an idealised boy, of course.

"Let us go there."

Arrived at the haystack, he sat down in the

shade of it, with William next to him, and drew out his violin.

He played for a quarter of an hour. Then he looked at William. William sat with a look of rapt attention on his face.

The musician could not know, of course, that in sheer boredom William had returned to his role of world potentate and was engaged in addressing his army on the eve of a great battle.

He played again, then again he looked at William.

"Another one," said William in a peremptory tone of voice that the musician took to be one of fervent appreciation.

He could not know, of course, that William was now a pirate, and was ordering his men to send yet another captured mariner along the plank.

He played again, then again looked at William. William's eyes were closed, as if in ecstasy.

He could not know, of course, that William was asleep.

He played again. The clock struck six. William sat up and heaved a sigh of relief.

"I've got to go home now," he said. "It's after my tea-time."

The musician glanced at him coldly and decided that the boy should make quite a different sort of remark in his memoirs.

They went back to the road in silence, and there parted – William to his home, and the musician to the station.

*

Mrs Bott, now on the verge of hysterics, went slowly down to the tent. To her amazement, a burst of loud laughter and clapping greeted her. She peeped in at the open flap. A Punch and Judy performance was in full and merry swing!

"I'm dreaming," she said. "Where's Zebra? Where did this thing come from?" Her eyes went to the noble lord. He was leaning forward in his seat, laughing uproariously.

After the first moment's stupefaction, everyone else had settled down to follow his example and enjoy the show. Signor Manelli was a born comedian. Toby carried his little sword with swagger.

"What's happened?" murmured Mrs Bott wildly. "I've gone potty."

But the performance was drawing to a close, amid a riot of applause. The noble lord had mounted the platform and was shaking Signor Manelli by the hand.

"Bravo!" he was saying. "I've not enjoyed anything so much for years. Not for *years*.

Now, look here, I want to book you for a party at my place in town next month. Have you a free date?"

It appeared that Signor Manelli had a free date. A fee was named, at which Signor Manelli almost fainted in sheer surprise. Suddenly the noble lord saw Mrs Bott.

"Ah!" he said genially. "Here is our hostess, to whom we owe this delightful entertainment."

Signor Manelli started forward to her eagerly. "And where is my little host?"

The mystery was suddenly clear to Mrs Bott. Botty must have engaged this man for her to fall back on, in case the Zebra person didn't turn up. It was just like Botty to do a thoughtful thing like that and not mention it.

"He's resting in the library," she said.

"I won't disturb him then," said Signor Manelli, "but give the dear little man my most grateful respects, and tell him that I shall never forget his kindness to me."

"Yes, I'll tell him," said Mrs Bott, and was at once surrounded by an eager crowd congratulating her on the success of her entertainment.

To her amazement, Mrs Bott discovered that her party had been a roaring success and that she was at last, "somebody".

When her guests had departed, she sought out her husband in the library.

"Oh Botty," she said hysterically, "how kind, how thoughtful of you to think of it. I shall never forget it – never."

He laid his hand gently on her shoulder. "You go and lie down, my dear," he said. "The excitement's gone to your head . . ."

The Browns were walking slowly homeward.

"I didn't see William there, apart from at first, did you?" said Ethel.

"He must have been there somewhere," said Mrs Brown. "I'm sure he loved the Punch and Judy show."

*

It was several months later. William sat at the table ostensibly engaged upon his homework. Mrs Brown was reading the paper and keeping up a desultory conversation with Ethel, who was embroidering a nightgown.

"It says that Punch and Judy is still all the rage in London," said Mrs Brown, "but that Signor Manelli, who started it, is taking no more engagements because he's going back to Italy. Do you remember him, dear? We saw him at that party of Mrs Bott's."

"Yes," said Ethel.

"And here's something about that Mr Zevrier, the musician that Mrs Bott once thought of having to her party, you know, before she decided to have the Punch and Judy . . ."

"What?" said Ethel absently.

"His book of memoirs has just been published. And it quotes an extract from it here. All about a musical child that he met when he was going to play at some sort of party and he stayed playing to it, and forgot the party and his fee and everything."

She looked up.

"I wonder – you know, people said that Mrs Bott had engaged him for her party, as well as the Punch and Judy show, and he didn't turn up. Could it have been *here* that he met this musical child?"

"What sort of child was it?" said Ethel.

"It quotes a description from the book," said Mrs Brown. "Here it is: 'He had deep-set, dark eyes and a pale, oval face, sensitive lips, and dark, curly hair. I saw at once that to him, as to me, music was the very breath of life.'"

Ethel laughed shortly. "No, it couldn't have been here," she said. "There isn't a child like *that* about here."

His head shielded by his hands in the attitude of one who wishes to devote himself entirely to study and shut out all disturbing influences, William grinned to himself . . .

Meet Just William
Richmal Crompton
Adapted by Martin Jarvis
Illustrated by Tony Ross

Just William as you've never seen him before!

A wonderful new series of *Just William* books, each containing four of
his funniest stories – all specially adapted for younger readers by Martin
Jarvis, the famous "voice of William" on radio and best-selling audio
cassette.

Meet Just William and the long-suffering Brown family, as well as the
Outlaws, Violet Elizabeth Bott and a host of other favourite characters
in these five hilarious books.

1. William's Birthday and Other Stories
2. William and the Hidden Treasure and Other Stories
3. William's Wonderful Plan and Other Stories
4. William and the Prize Cat and Other Stories
5. William's Haunted House and Other Stories